Lizzie
McGuire

Su

$4.99

1st ed.

FAMILY

Survival Guide

FAMILY

Based on the series created by Terri Minsky

Watch it on

DISNEY PRESS

VOLO

New York

Printed in the United States of America

First Edition
1 3 5 7 9 10 8 6 4 2

Library of Congress Catalog Card Number on file.

ISBN: 0-7868-4665-8
For more Disney Press fun, visit www.disneybooks.com
Visit DisneyChannel.com

Contents

Why YOU Need ME

Hi there! I'm Lizzie—but you already knew that, right? I'm here to help you survive the most difficult job in the world—being part of a family.

If your family is anything like mine, you'll know family life is mixed up! Your parents embarrass you ... but you love 'em just the same! Your Gammy is weird ... but she's cool as well! Your little brother drives you crazy ... but it's illegal to sell him. Some life!

As if I could even give Matt away, let alone make a profit.

So do you want to find out if your family's normal? Want to be able to translate what your dad is saying? Perhaps learn to get along with your irritating little brother or sister and get tips on how to win your parents' trust? Then read my essential survival guide – and I promise your home life will be every bit as peaceful as mine.

My family?
Peaceful?
HA-HA-HA-HA
HA-HA-HA!

First off, it's good to know where you came from (so you know who to blame). Take a look at my family tree....

The McGuire Family Tree

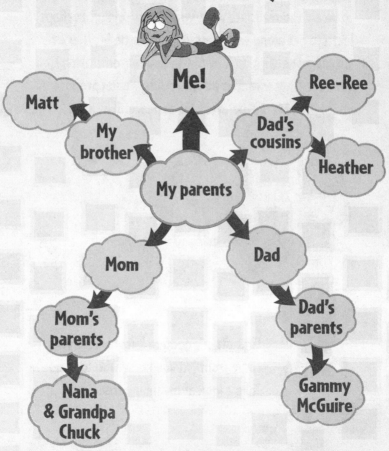

Me

The head of the household...
kinda. Check out page 50 for
more about the only sane McGuire.

Matt

What can be said about Matt that
criminal psychologists haven't already
covered? See page 51 for the 4-1-1.

Mom

How embarrassing can one woman
be? Check out page 12 for the
awful truth.

Dad

His rapping makes
dogs howl. Check it
out on page 13.

Cousin Ree-Ree and Cousin Heather

Uh, these two are distant
cousins... *real* distant.
Get the facts on page 72.

Gammy McGuire

Oh, sweet Gammy! A wonderful
lady, but sadly, one sandwich
short of a picnic. See page 73
for why.

Nana and Grandpa Chuck

Anyone else's grandmother like
surfing and trips to Vegas?

 Mom

Name: Jo McGuire

Aka: Mom, or Tallulah

Bio: She's a one-woman embarrassment factory. Mom is a real pro. Are all moms like this or is it just mine? Does your mom want to talk to you about your feelings all the time? Mine sure does. Still, she manages to be pretty cool despite all that, and she's always there for me.

Most likely to say: "Hey, Lizzie – have you seen the hairbrush? Oh, and by the way ..."

Least likely to say: "The only way to win Ethan's heart is to get a tattoo."

Weak spots: Me being thoughtless – I sometimes forget that she's *not* just out to embarrass me, and that I really need her.

Best moment: Taking the rap for me when we TP'd the boys' tent on the class trip. Go, Mom!

Worst moment: Having her feelings hurt by yours truly when we were underwear shopping.

Could surprise you by: Telling you your dad owes the IRS $618 million (not true!), or that your grandparents are splitting up.

Too much information!

Survival strategy: Learn to live with bouts of public shame. And love her, anyway!

Dad

Name: Sam McGuire

Aka: Dad, the Real Sam Shady

Bio: Dad's more laid-back than Mom, so you can get more past him, most of the time. He looks like an adult but he's done a lot of really weird stuff, like soapbox racing, hanging out in the Mattcave, or being starstruck by the *Uncle Wendell Show*.

Most likely to say: "And where do you think you're going dressed like *that*?"

Least likely to say: "You should get your belly button pierced this weekend. Oh, and just come back from that party when you feel like it."

Weak spots: His obsession with sports memorabilia, and Mom's laser-beam death glare.

Best moment: Skateboarding along a Mile of Death track that Matt set up. No broken bones! (The nose isn't a bone, is it?)

Worst moment: The rap he did for me at my eleventh birthday party. And me with no rock to crawl under.

Could surprise you by: Showing you he really cares... even if he is terrible at starting those father–daughter chats.

Survival strategy: Distract him – get him talking about Walter Peyton.

You don't need to know who he is... trust me!

The Dad Dictionary

Part I

Dads have two functions in life:

1. To look after you and protect you from harm
2. To mortally embarrass you by pretending to be cool

Only they don't say "cool" – they say "hip" or "groovy." I think it's their way of feeling in touch with the "youth of today," as they call us. What*ever*.

So half the time they're trying to prove they're still "with it" (don't ask), that they can "cut a rug" . . .

Are you getting all of this?!

. . . or that they're "down with the kids." (Ow. Ow. Ow.) If they say stuff that makes zero sense, you need my handy *Dad Dictionary* to figure it out.

◉ 8-Track

Not sure. Some kind of sports arena, maybe?

◉ Groovy

Cool (but not as cool as "cool" – obviously).

◉ Cut a rug

Hmm, something to do with damaged carpet?

◉ Where's the beef?

Some kind of nutritional catchphrase from the 1930s?
May have been Abraham Lincoln's campaign slogan.

The Mom Dictionary

Part I

Moms also have their very own language. The basic rule is this: they don't necessarily mean what they say. Here are a few examples:

She says: "Lizzie, have you seen the hairbrush?"

She means: "I am using a lame excuse to get into your bedroom and start a very long and embarrassing conversation about your feelings."

She says: "I'm not angry with you, Lizzie, I'm just disappointed."

She means: "I am angry with you."

She says: "It's your decision, Lizzie – you do whatever your conscience tells you to."

She means: "Unless it's the wrong decision. Then *I'll* tell you what to do."

Quiz: All About Dad!

He's taller than you are, he likes sports, and he says, "You're not going out dressed like that!" a lot. But did you know there might be more to your dad than that? It's true! Some people even believe dads had their own lives before you and I were born.

Yeah, and if you believe *that*, there's a bridge in Brooklyn I wanna sell you. . . .

Every now and then, my dad takes me out to dinner for some father-daughter bonding . . . so I know a lot of stuff about him. Take my patented quiz, and get to know the man behind the phrase: "I don't know — ask your mother."

Fill in your answers here!

1. What is your dad's middle name?

_____

2. How old is he?

_____

3. What's his favorite
   sports team?

_____

Ancient is
not an acceptable
answer, however
true it might be.

4. How did he meet your mom?

_____

_____

_____

_____

5. What's his job?

_____

_____

_____

_____

6. Who is his hero?

_____

7. What does he like to do on weekends?

_____

8. Who is his best friend?

_____

9. Who is his favorite child?

_____

Joke!
That was a joke!
(But it *is* me,
right?)

Now check with your dad to find out how many questions
you got right. If you got seven or more correct, you are
one doting daughter!

The Dad Dictionary

Part II

 He says: "And what do you think you're wearing?"
(Don't say, "a miniskirt" – he's not actually looking
for an answer.)

He means: "I don't want boys looking at you.
Stay at home forever and play with your dolls."

He says: "Far out!"

He means: "Cool."

He says: "Ask your mom."

He means: "I'm a little scared of my wife."

The Mom Dictionary

Part II

She says: "Don't make me come up there!"

She means: "I'm too tired to yell at you."

She says: "I want us to be friends."

She means: "I'm the kind of friend who can also tell you when to go to bed."

She says: "Is this dress too young for me?"

She means: "Say something flattering or your allowance is history!"

Nice Stuff You Can Do for Your Parents

I know I go on about how embarrassing my folks can be, but they're pretty cool, really. And let's face it, they have a tough job.

My parents have to look after Matt — there are prison sentences way shorter than that.

Sometimes it's easy to forget how much they do for you — they put a roof over your head, and give you free food, clothes, and CDs. And what do they get in return? A grouchy "I dunno" when they ask what you did at school that day.

We get a pretty sweet deal – so why not do something to make their day every once in a while? Check out my suggestions:

◉ Go shopping with your mom

Okay, so she might pick out clothes you wouldn't even wear in the dark, but she'll have a great time doing it.

◉ Make breakfast

It's time they were forced to sit down and eat *your* food. But don't attempt anything that says soufflé.

Yeah, stick to what you know. Like toast.

Read a book together

Like *The Orchids and Gumbo Poker Club*, which I read for English class. The important thing is, you can spend time talking about it.

Treat your dad to a slice of pizza

My dad and I do this from time to time. It doesn't have to be fancy — and he'll love it. Trust me.

◉ Write them a letter

Sometimes you can't quite say what you mean when you're talking to your parents. But if you take the time to write down how much they mean to you, they'll remember it forever. It won't break the bank, either! See page 41 for my letter-writing tips.

◉ Do your own laundry . . . without being asked

Your parents can spend the extra time with their feet up.

Trust Me,
I'm a Professional!

Okay, so I'm actually just a teenager who sleeps with Mr. Snuggles under my arm — but what's so wrong with that?

Research shows that more than 65 percent of all prowlers are terrified of small, fluffy pigs. Fact!

It's a tough business, growing up, and a lot of the time you get treated like a baby when all you want is to be an adult.

Face it, deep down, your parents still see you as Liddle-Widdle-Teeny-Smileyface-Babykins... or, like, whatever.

Like the time I wanted to babysit Matt. It's not that I actually wanted to look after the little pest; I just wanted my folks to realize that I could be responsible. Okay, so he wouldn't do anything I asked him to and he made a mess all over the place. Then we ended up thinking Dad was a prowler and we nearly killed him before getting him arrested, so maybe that's not the best example...

But do you see where I'm going here?
Sometimes you just need to be treated like an
adult, or you can't see the point in growing up.
So how do you get your folks to loosen up and
stop treating you like a kid?

Stop *acting* like a kid

Hey, I'm not joking here! Girls who freak out at their little
brothers, or throw a tantrum when it's time for bed, do
not impress parents. Try to act calm and your parents will
notice – honestly!

Ask for more chores or run errands

No, really – still not joking! Show them you are responsible
and can be trusted with stuff. First, take on the garbage . . .
next, the world!

Always come home on time

Can't stress this one enough. Always come back when your parents say – *always*. Get a rep for reliability, and your folks will freak less when you ask to do the things you want to do. It's all points in the Parent Bank.

Ask for a part-time job

This is another good one for brownie points, and babysitting can be a good choice ... after all, kids are the most important things in the house, right?

Except to my dad. In his case, it's his sports memorabilia.

So there you go — try out my handy tips, and pretty soon you'll have enough brownie points to go to all-night parties and watch R-rated films.* Just remember, it's pretty cool to be a kid (you get to avoid a lot of really boring stuff!), and it's pretty scary to be an adult, so before you head off into the sunset, make sure you know where your Mr. Snuggles is!

*Strike that and change to: enough brownie points to go to a sleepover at Miranda's, and watch *Pocahontas* until it's time for bed.

Book Smart!

Have you ever wondered how dads know so
much about stuff? How they know the exact
moment to say the most embarrassing thing?
Why they're drawn to power tools? And how
they instinctively know when you're trying to
sneak out wearing a miniskirt?

Well, I have the answers – they're all written down in
The Big Book of Dads. No kidding! I've jotted down the
main points, and believe me, they explain everything....

The Big Book of Dads

Chapter One
Making Your Daughter Happy

Dancing Every girl loves to see her father dance, so dance every chance you get. She'll be especially thrilled if you do it in front of her friends, while loudly encouraging her to dance with you.

Rapping There's only one thing better than dancing, and that's rapping! Show that you're "down with the kids" by "busting" some "mad rhymes" every now and again. Don't forget to wear a baseball cap — sideways.

Clothes Daughters need constant reassurance about their clothes, so don't let her go out without some comment on what she's wearing — otherwise she'll feel neglected. The more constructive criticism the better! Try out the following phrases:

"You're not going out dressed like *that*!"

"Is that a skirt or just a big belt?"

"And where do you think you're going in that outfit?"

Chapter Two
Your Daughter and Dating

Your daughter's first date is a landmark occasion, so be prepared. Here are some ready-made phrases to use when your daughter asks if she can go on her very first date with a boy:

"Over my dead body!"

"Sure, where are we all going?
I'm free Saturday."

"No dating boys until
after you're married."

My Bad!

You can be the most law-abiding girl in the world, but sometimes you might end up accidentally, y'know, breaking the rules.

Like that time I really really wanted to go see that film *Vesuvius*, but Mom and Dad said I was too young. I kinda accidentally ended up going anyway...but I got busted in the end.

And how! Appearing on TV saving someone's life? Nice low profile, McGuire!

And when you're busted, you've gotta take the heat. Matt's pretty good at this – he's in trouble so often he's grounded until October … 2009! Here are my tips on how to survive if you've broken the rules....

Say you're sorry

Your parents may be angry with you, or disappointed, or even worried. Apologizing will show them you understand that you've upset them.

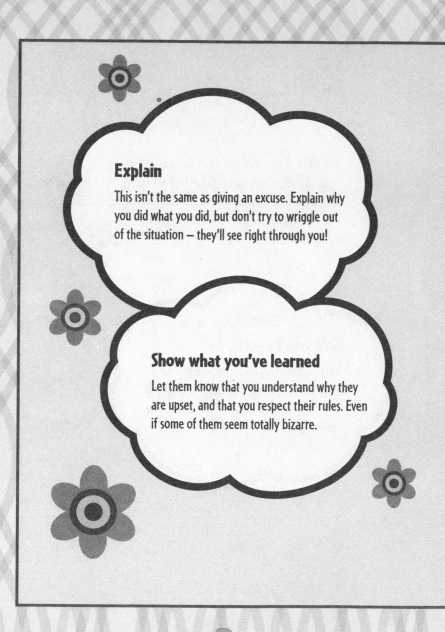

Explain

This isn't the same as giving an excuse. Explain why you did what you did, but don't try to wriggle out of the situation – they'll see right through you!

Show what you've learned

Let them know that you understand why they are upset, and that you respect their rules. Even if some of them seem totally bizarre.

Accept the rap

If you agree that you've broken the rules and that there will be consequences, you'll actually feel better. Treat it as a learning experience rather than something really unfair.

And next time, make sure you don't get caught! *Joke!* I was just joking . . . . Geez.

United Mom Front

If your mom wanders into your room "looking for something," chances are, what she really wants is to talk about your "feelings"... *again*. So are there guidelines that all moms have to follow? Is there a master plan? There is! After all, how could everyone's mom act the same unless they were all using the same strategy? I found all I needed to know in *The Mother/Daughter Handbook* — pretty chilling stuff.

The Mother/Daughter Handbook

Chapter One
Your Daughter's Blossoming Life

Your daughter is entering into a time of great change – both emotionally and physically. It's very important to reassure her during this difficult time by talking fully and frankly about how she feels. Nonstop. All the time. Leave no topic unturned – your daughter will appreciate your candor. Topics of conversation could include:

- Boys

- My little girl is growing up

- Would her friends like to come over and talk about their feelings, too?

Chapter Two
Sustaining Your
Mind-Reading Abilities

Every mother knows the importance of reading her child's mind.* And although we all possess basic mind-reading powers, we must continue to enhance this useful tool. Beginning next month, the new edition of *Practical Mind-Reading and You* will be distributed for general use. Remember, this guide is especially useful for dealing with the following issues:

* Nasty stain on the rug

* No appetite at dinner

* Broken window

* Severe sucking up

* Do not stand next to Matt McGuire of Hillridge Elementary while using your mind-reading powers. His thoughts will make you very tired.

Write On!

Now, you may not believe this, but sometimes I get a little tongue-tied. Just once in a while – hardly ever, really....

Like, only whenever I stand up to Kate, talk to Ethan, try to sneak a white lie past my mom, or have to speak in class. Apart from all that, I'm pretty good!

Sometimes I don't manage to get across exactly what I want to say to my parents, because being a kid can be as tough as Gammy McGuire's meat loaf. So here's a survival tip for you – if you've got a problem, or are feeling down, why not write your mom or dad a letter? It'll help you sort your feelings out, and you'll be able to tell them exactly what you think! Check out my advice....

Dos:

* **DO** ... keep the letter short and sweet — that way it'll be more memorable.

* **DO** ... plan what you want to say — this is your big chance!

* **DO** ... tell them exactly how you feel if you're unhappy about something.

* **DO** ... offer a suggestion about how to improve things. They'll appreciate it, even if they don't agree with it.

* **DO** ... tell them you love them. We might think those words are embarrassing, but they're true, and parents love to hear them!

Don'ts:

❋ **DON'T**...write it in a secret code.

❋ **DON'T**...put your last name on it. If they don't know who you are by now, they should be ashamed!

❋ **DON'T**...write it straight after a fight – take time to calm down first.

❋ **DON'T**...turn it into a big list of gripes. That'll get you nowhere.

Parent Ping-Pong

We've all done it — played one parent
against the other, right? I mean, the way
I see it is this: you gotta use a certain tool
for a certain job. When I want to go on a
date, for example, I ask Mom, not Dad....

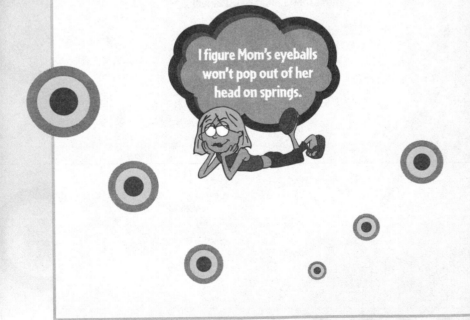

I figure Mom's eyeballs
won't pop out of her
head on springs.

...but if I want money for
new clothes, I ask Dad.

But I'd probably
tell him I was buying
a sensible wool
sweater.

Sometimes it's like a Get Out of Jail Free card! One
parent says "no"? Then try the other! Of course, as
with any good idea, there's a downside....

Good things about Parent Ping-Pong:

❇ You get two tries at everything!

❇ Pester power works — keep at it and one of them might give in!

❇ You've known them so long that you can guess who's gonna say "no" and who might say "yes," depending on what the question is.

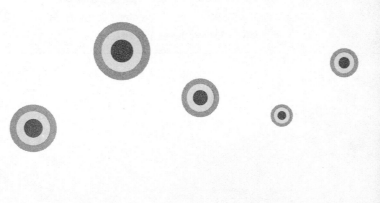

Bad things about Parent Ping-Pong:

 They always find out. Always. Bit of a problem there.

The funny thing is, they're never that pleased about it. Go figure....

 And there's always the outside possibility that you might end up feeling bad about it... just a little.

Don't Even Go There!

Despite their lovable exterior, moms often seem like they are secretly on a mission from Planet Humiliation to make you spontaneously combust from sheer embarrassment. So watch out for these little gems. . . .

In front of your friends:

"Oh, don't you look adorable in that top!"

(No, Mom — newborn kittens are adorable . . . I'm cool, you hear me?)

At the bus stop:

"Sweetie pie! You forgot your lunch!"

Say it a bit louder, Mom — the people in the next state didn't quite hear you.

Anywhere, anytime:

"I remember *my* first crush when I was a girl. . . ."

(Suddenly, I have to be somewhere else. Fast.)

In front of your little brother's friends:

"I know you really love your brother, deep down."

Yeah, so deep down it's neighbors with the lost city of Atlantis!

In your room:

"Now, let me know when you want to talk about the birds and the bees...."

(Sure, how about June 24, 2036?)

At the dinner table:

"Your dad and I are still very much in love." *Smooch!*

(Oh, please – I'm eating!)

Lizzie

Name: Lizzie McGuire

Aka: Sweet Potato (but only my mom calls me that).

Bio: Hey, where to start? I'm the oldest child in your average family: Mom's obsessed with my "feelings," Dad's obsessed with garden gnomes, and my little brother's obsessed with ruining my life. You know, just the usual.

Most likely to say: "Mom! Matt's doing it again!"

Least likely to say: "Wow, what a well-adjusted family I've got."

Weak spots: Dad's "Special Daughter Dinners"; going underwear shopping with my mom; sweater blackmail from Gammy McGuire.

Best Moment: Realizing that, no matter how much they might embarrass me, my mom and dad really do love me a lot.

Embarrassed? Me? Only on days ending in 'y'.

Worst Moment: Realizing that, no matter how many times I suggest it, my mom and dad aren't going to release Matt back into the wild.

Could surprise you by: Spontaneously combusting from sheer humiliation. It could happen!

Survival Strategy: Just be nice to me!

Matt

Name: Matt McGuire

Aka: Mattman, the Amazing Matt (what he calls himself), the Creature from the Black Latrine (what I call him).

Bio: If life is a bowl of cherries, he's a cherry-eating slug. I mean, I must've done something really, really bad in a past life to deserve him.

Most likely to say: "I bet I can eat twelve candy bars without throwing up!"

Least likely to say: "I really look up to you, Lizzie."

Weak spots: Mom's laser-beam death stare; bribes (candy and trading cards are acceptable currency); and Melina's pranks.

Best moment: Being psychic? Becoming a rock star? Appearing in a TV commercial? Running Hillridge's most successful hangout? You choose.

Is it me, or is crime definitely paying around here?

Worst moment: Well, I think for me, all things considered, it was him being *born*. It pretty much went downhill for me immediately after that.

Could surprise you by: Saying he loves his big sister.

Survival strategy: Avoid, avoid, avoid. Or if that fails —

Q: **What do you call a hundred little brothers locked in the basement?**

A: **A good start!**

Little Brothers & Evolution

There's a lot of controversy over little brothers, and most people are completely divided about how they see them. Some people think little brothers are unholy agents of evil . . . whereas other people think of them as stinky, revolting mutants. So there's a lot of disagreement on the subject.

Hmm, unholy agents of evil or stinky, revolting mutants — I do love a good debate.

So, where do little brothers fit on the evolutionary scale?

The Evolutionary Scale

Where does your little brother (or sister!) fit in?

People

You know, normal people like you and me, and Ethan Craft. Human beings who can eat politely and operate a telephone. Okay, maybe not Ethan....

Monkeys

Our closest cousins, but still a real long way away from little brothers....

Reptiles

Little brothers have a *lot* in common with reptiles, but they're lower still....

Leeches

Gross, slimy parasites that attach themselves to you when you least expect it. But at least leeches don't drive their sisters nuts all the time.

Bacteria

They make you sick, they're pretty much indestructible, and they dirty up kitchen surfaces. Sound familiar? But there's a creature that's even lower down on the scale....

Little Brothers!

Right at the bottom of the heap — exactly where they belong.

People Matt Has Blamed for Bad Stuff

- the Evil Shoe Baron
- the Amazing Mattman
- the Amazing Mattman's evil twin
- Gordo
- a chimpanzee
- Mrs. Mendchick from down the street

He Has Done

- ( ) John Boy Walton from *The Waltons*
- ( ) Cousin Ree-Ree
- ( ) Thomas Edison
- ( ) Gammy McGuire
- ( ) Melina
- ( ) me

Can't We Just Get Along?

Okay, so you've got the second-worst sibling in the whole world....

Three guesses for who's got the worst. Anyone?

What's the best way to deal with siblings who bug you all the time? Superglue their shoes to the floor? Donate them to science? Put them up for auction?

If you're not careful, the situation can descend into an all-out household war. Matt and I argue all the time. We argued so much one day, our parents took away all our stuff so we wouldn't have anything to argue over!

Camping out with your bro on your bedroom floor, with only a sleeping bag ... wow, why don't they have *that* ride at Disney World?

But you've gotta learn to roll with the punches. Here's my handy guide to keeping the earsplitting fights to a minimum....

Trade Off!

There's gotta be something that your sibling does that drives you crazy — something that you just can't stand! Me? I hate it when Matt hides my shoes just before I go out....

Go barefoot? That's so 1970s.

...and Matt hates it when I put open cans of tuna under his bed.

So, what to do? Why not make up a list of three things that drive you crazy, and trade 'em? You promise not to do stuff on their list; they promise not to do stuff on your list. Everyone wins! And the first one to stop gets *two* cans of tuna under their bed....

Chill Out!

Your sibs can drive you so nuts that you're always on Red Alert. What I'm talking about here is de-stressing. If you take a little time out and chill for a few minutes, you may find that you don't go so ballistic the next time they do something.

And remember, stinky sibs just love to get a rise out of you. If you don't get wound up, they don't enjoy it so much. What better reason could you have to stay super cool?

Ms. Innocent?

Let's take a look at you for a minute, shall we? Your sibs may drive you completely nuts with their behavior, but are you sure you're not doing stuff too? Come on . . . just a little? I know I do — and Miranda says she hides her brother's stuff all the time just to watch his eyes go around like pinwheels.

Seriously, though, think about how you could be adding to the Sib War, and maybe even think about keeping the peace for a while....

How about two minutes? What? Longer than that?

Call in the Cavalry!

Finally, don't forget that your folks want to see you two getting along! They can help – if you let them. It's not a question of being a tattletale, more like calling in a consultant to help you through a tricky problem.

Your parents don't want to take sides, though, so don't bring them on board if that's what you're after. All they want is a cease-fire! So why not get a parent and a sibling around the campfire and see if you can't sing a happier tune?

Yeah, just make sure your dad doesn't *actually* sing.

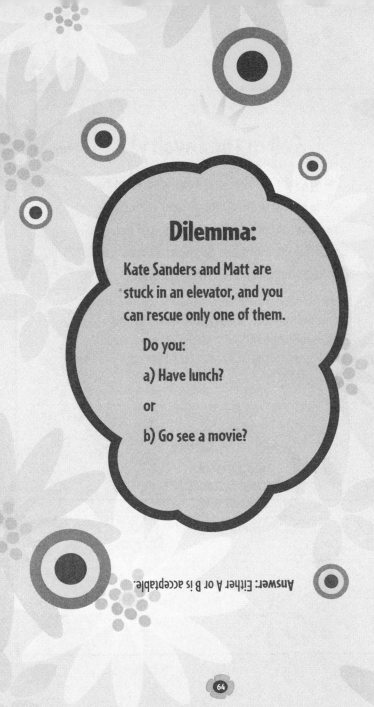

Dilemma:

Kate Sanders and Matt are stuck in an elevator, and you can rescue only one of them.

Do you:

a) Have lunch?

or

b) Go see a movie?

Answer: Either A or B is acceptable.

64

Brain Teaser

The Abominable Snowman; the Loch Ness Monster; and a nice, clean, well-behaved little brother are at a crossroads. In the middle of the intersection is a fifty-dollar bill. If they all start walking at the same time, who will get to the money first?

Answer: Nobody. They're all FIGMENTS OF YOUR IMAGINATION!

Little Brother Dictionary

No one really wants to talk to my little brother – sometimes not even his best friend . . . but it is good to know what the little creep is up to. That's why it's important to be able to make sense of what he's saying. Unlike normal people, little brother s speak in code, so if you're going to survive having a kid brother, you'd better learn to speak his lingo, because he may be talking about you!

Take note of these phrases – they might just save your sanity, and they'll definitely save you tons of trouble when he tries to blame that broken window on you!

He says: "I didn't do it!"

Translation: He did it.

He says: "I didn't do it – I don't know what you're talking about!"

Translation: He did it, but he's not sure which crime you've uncovered.

He says: "Hey, Mom – you're looking real pretty today!"

Translation: He has replaced all the furniture with sculptures made from neighborhood trash.

He says: "Dad, isn't it about time you and Lizzie had another father-daughter dinner?"

Translation: He has repainted the family car in the style of Picasso.

He says: "A pet chimpanzee has eaten my homework."

Translation: A pet chimpanzee has eaten his homework.

The one truth Matt tells, and it's about naughty Fredo the Chimp escaping from his owners. Go figure!

🌼 **He says:** "Why, Lizzie, you're looking radiant today!"

Translation: He has a high fever and is hallucinating. Call a doctor immediately.

🌼 **He says:** "Lizzie, can you come in here?"

Translation: He has a large bucket of chocolate pudding/water/flour in a bucket over the door.

🌼 **He says:** "Lizzie, it's the phone for you — a Miss I. M. Smelly?"

Translation: The boy has a criminally lame sense of humor.

Lizzie:
"Hey, Matt, how many little brothers does it take to change a lightbulb?"

Matt:
"None — that lightbulb isn't broken! I wasn't anywhere near it! I've got witnesses! MOM! LIZZIE'S PICKING ON ME!"

Ways to Get Revenge on Your Little Brother

- Get him a subscription to *Knit Your Way to Happiness* and have it delivered to his classroom.

- Swap his shampoo for honey.

- Tell him you love him.

- Call the circus and tell them you know where their escaped warthog is (by the time they notice the difference, they'll be in the next state).

Cousin Ree-Ree & Cousin Heather

Cousin Ree-Ree is really my father's cousin, so I guess that makes him my, uh, second cousin, or something like that. Anyway, we see Cousin Ree-Ree every once in a while, but he's a pretty bad influence on Dad, so Mom's not so hot on having him visit too often. Hey, it's a shame she doesn't feel the same way about Matt!

Cousin Heather actually *is* my cousin, but we don't see each other very often — especially since Gordo admitted he used to have a crush on her way back when. How weird is that? Well, it's weird, anyway.

Gammy McGuire

Name: Mrs. McGuire

Aka: Gammy

Bio: A really sweet old lady, who I love a lot. She's bighearted, always remembers birthdays, and is really kind. I just wouldn't let her out on her own, that's all!

Most likely to say: "Oh, is it your birthday again, Matt? I'd better get my purse."

Least likely to say: "On reflection, Lizzie, I don't think that unicorn sweater I sent is very *you*."

Weakness: Whew, where to start? Gammy gets confused by a lot of stuff — calendars ... bus schedules ... cutlery ... post office lines ... sidewalks ... and which street she lives on. But, hey, nothing important!

Best moment: Giving me a unicorn sweater — not that I realized this at the time, but now I know it's not the present that's important, it's how much love it's sent with. (I'm still never gonna wear it, though!)

Worst moment: Her birthday being on the same day as the Pool Party. That was a tough one for me— it was pretty conflicting to choose between family and friends. ...

So conflicting I was picking out *bathing suits* ...

Could surprise you by: Being sharper than she actually looks ... or looking sharper than she actually is. No one really knows which one it is for sure.

Survival strategy: Enjoy the attention!

Gammy McGuire's Xmas Blunders

We all love Gammy — and Gammy loves us. But sometimes Gammy isn't entirely *there*, and her Christmas presents prove it. While I'd never say it to her face, some of them are downright weird. Take a look at the gifts she's given me over the last few years. (I keep reminding myself that it's the thought that counts!)

2003 Fourteen pairs of sweat socks

2002 Thirteen pairs of sweat socks

2001 Twelve pairs of sw . . . see where I'm going with this?

I don't even like to sweat!

1999 A unicorn sweater and a book titled *You Are Only as Young as Your Spleen*

1998 Magic Markers, a fake mustache kit, and a lemon

1997

(April) Candy

(June) More candy

(July) Some candy wrappers

(Nov) A letter apologizing for forgetting to send me any candy

My advice on grandparents? Love 'em while you got 'em . . . and, hey, you can never have too many pairs of sweat socks. Or something like that.

Is That Normal?

Do all dads like sports so much? Can all moms read your mind? Does everyone's Nana like skydiving and playing blackjack in Vegas?

Let's face it, from time to time, we've all wondered if our family is, well, normal — and here's where you get to find out! Take the patented Lizzie McGuire *Is My Family Normal or Are They Just a Circus Act?* test and you can wave your worries aside. Maybe.

Take a look through the questions, fill in your answers, and see how your family scores.

1 You and your family are going on a vacation. Where are you headed?

(a) Paris, France
Ooh-la-la, it's expensive, but it'll be a once-in-a-lifetime trip that everyone will always remember.

(b) Florida
The Keys are great at this time of year, and really, who doesn't love going to the beach?

(c) Grubby Longjohn's Gulch
It's a really long drive to get there, it's really creepy when you arrive, and nothing works properly.

What? Our two weeks are up already? But I was just getting used to that smell.

2 It's Halloween — the scariest night of the year! Whoooo! What do your folks do while you're out at the school party?

a Go to bed early — after all, Halloween is one of the few nights they get a break from their little devils.

b Make some popcorn and watch scary movies on cable until they get so scared, they can't go to sleep.

c Attack Mr. and Mrs. Sanchez by pelting them with flour and eggs, then hosing them down — all for no apparent reason!

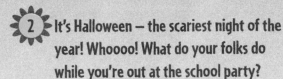

Sometimes I wonder how I have any self-respect left at all.

3 Your dad and brother want to get to know each other better. How do they spend some time bonding?

a They take a day to go fishin' in the old creek — there ain't too many fish in there, but that leaves plenty o' time for jawin'.

b They go for a hike in the hills. The clean air and great views are perfect for father-son bonding.

c They spend the afternoon causing seven kinds of pain to each other filming a martial-arts movie.

A truth for the ages: dads are weird.

4 Your mother comes with you on a school trip to the woods. Arrrgh – Code Blue! But what is the *most* embarrassing thing she does on the trip?

(a) She's really strict with all your friends, and they start calling her Commandant McGuire.

(b) She keeps saying stuff like "Don't forget to watch out for poison ivy when nature calls" to everyone.

(c) She gets caught in a water gun attack by the boys, and retaliates by TP-ing their tent. Then she gets busted! (And takes the rap!)

Wisdom doesn't always come with age, I guess.

5 How does your family like to spend a quiet afternoon?

a Resting in the shade, drinking peppermint tea, and watching the sunset.

b Sitting in front of the fireplace, reading newspapers, and talking about the day's current events.

c Building a Mile of Death skateboard track, which lands your dad in the ER.

Watch out for the flaming hoop, Dad!

So, how did your family do? Worried that they're weird, or confident that they're conventional? Check out how to score:

Mostly a's

You're more like the Waltons than the Simpsons! If you guys are for real, you're probably not even reading this; you're sitting around making a patchwork quilt!

Mostly b's

Totally average. So normal, in fact, that it's a bit creepy. But don't worry. I don't think anyone will notice – just as long as you stay inside the house.

Mostly c's

Congratulations – you're an honorary McGuire! In fact, we might even be related! Your dad's name isn't Ree-Ree by any chance, is it?

Q: What do you call a family that gets into more embarrassing situations than Larry Tudgeman?

A: The McGuires. Obviously.

Lizzie's Emergency Survival Tips

- Never turn your back on your little brother when he's holding a handful of chocolate pudding.

- Under no circumstances ask your dad about "the old days."

- The candy at your grandma's is very old and just ornamental.

- Moms do not think getting a tattoo is cool – not even a tattoo that says "Mother" on it.

- All cousins are weird. Each and every one.

Surviving Family Holidays

No matter how difficult your family is, you can always escape, right? Well, not always. There are a few times a year when family togetherness is unavoidable — the holidays. It could be Easter, Christmas, summer vacation, or anything else your family celebrates — even Halloween.

Long, hot, summer vacation car trip with Matt, anyone?

Take a look at my guaranteed guide to surviving....

Christmas

What is it?

A heartwarming winter holiday during which the whole family gets together to swap gifts, enjoy one another's company, and relax in front of the fireplace – sharing those special family moments.

What is it *really*?

Spending too much on gifts, getting lame presents from your brother, arguing over what to watch on TV, having to spend time with relatives you don't know. And fruitcake. Way too much fruitcake.

Fruitcake I don't do. *Cake* cake I do.

Danger areas:

Cooking... Don't get involved. Kitchens become war zones during Christmas. Avoid!

Cousins... You don't know 'em, you've got nothing to say to 'em, but suddenly they're in your house!

TV... You will not get to watch what you want. Live with it.

Survival tips:

You've gotta focus on what's really important. It doesn't matter what you do, or where you are, just as long as you're with the people you care about.

Most likely to happen:

Bickering leading to a giant family argument, which everyone then forgets about until next year.

Least likely to happen:

Matt being a "good little boy" beyond Christmas Day. Hey, Santa – take note!

Threat to survival:

Huge – but any holiday with gifts can't be all bad.

Halloween

What is it?

A chance for the whole family to get together and enjoy some chills and thrills, showing you that although some stuff might be scary, it can still be fun if you stick together.

What is it *really*?

As far as I can tell, it's just a really big excuse to beg for candy. Which is good. But the bad part of it is . . . your mom and dad. They think it's cute when you dress up, and they may even want to dress up themselves! You know how embarrassing your dad can be? Think it's gonna be better if he's dressed like Vegas Elvis?

Danger areas:

Parents enjoy the fun too much — they might even come with you to chaperone your trick-or-treating . . . but it's really so they can dress up and embarrass you to death. Just in case they go unnoticed, they tend to shout stuff like: "Isn't Lizzie cute as a zombie?" to all their friends. Real loud. And telling Matt that he's *expected* to behave in a mischievous, evil way is pretty much the dumbest thing you could do.

Survival tips:

Your best bet? Hole up in the house and have a scary movie fest. That way at least none of your family can embarrass you outside . . . they'll just continue to do it at home. And maybe watching *The Return of the Colossal, Radioactive, Undead Monster from Limbo* will keep everyone nice and quiet.

Until Matt wakes up everyone in the house with his bad dreams, of course!

Most likely to happen:

Stomachache from all that candy!

Least likely to happen:

Convincing my mom *not* to wear a vampire costume.

Threat to survival:

Huge — do I need to say it again? Parents. In. Costume.

Easter

What is it?

Easter is the other time of the year when the whole family gathers together for a big love-in — the only differences are that there's no tree, no turkey, and no presents....

What is it *really*?

Chocolate! White chocolate! Dark chocolate! Chocolate eggs, bunnies, ducks, giraffes! Choco-choco-chocolate!

Is that clear enough?

Danger areas:

Try this on for size: here's your little brother – and here's your little brother on a two-week sugar rush. Have you got any idea what you're letting yourself in for? A Tasmanian devil has less energy! And he'll use it all for purest evil, believe me.

Survival tips:

Take cover. Hole yourself up in your room, bolt the door, and wait for Hurricane Bro to wear itself out.

Most likely to happen:

Hyperactivity from all that sugar.

Least likely to happen:

Healthy eating and no temper tantrums.

Threat to survival:

Big – I never thought I'd say this, but a girl *can* have too much chocolate.

Summer Vacation

What is it?

A swell time for the family to get out on the open road for excitement, fun, and family bonding.

What is it *really*?

A stifling time when family members get on each other's nerves, cooped up in a car for what feels like several years of bickering, soaring temperatures, and driving to Disappointment, Nebraska, to see the world's largest ball of twine.

I guess what I'm saying is that I'm not a fan.

Danger areas:

Sweltering heat, not being able to escape your little brother, car sickness, terminal boredom, listening to your parents sing show tunes, and the possibility of having to see *Grubby Longjohn's Old Tyme Revue*....

Survival tips:

Try sleeping. If you work really hard at it, you can sleep for as many as eighteen hours a day. And don't forget a Walkman so you can drown out everyone else. Also, never agree to play "I Spy" from a moving car. It just doesn't work.

Most likely to happen:

Nothing. Then more nothing. But then, just when you least expect it . . . nothing.

Least likely to happen:

Your dad pulling into the airport and saying: "Surprise – we're going to Disney World, after all!"

Threat to survival:

Total – am I making myself clear?

Lizzie McGuire, Survival Guru, Signing Out

So that's it! Everything you need to know in order to survive family life with a clear conscience and a roomful of lousy Christmas presents. If you're still reading, then I guess some of my tips are paying off! Just do as I say, and your family life will be calmer, more relaxed, and super chilled.

So good luck with your family — if yours is anything like mine, you'll need it!

Stay in touch!

Love,
Lizzie